Dedication

This book is dedicated to the children of the world. My goal is for them to see themselves through my creations. I hope that everyone who reads it experiences the magic and identifies with the characters. I do not want any child to feel left out.

Acknowledgements

I want to thank my illustrator, Ohana Tozato, for bringing my vision to life. My love for children, animals, and the universe inspired me to create this story. I wanted to share this love with millions of people around the world.

Loyal, Liam, and Lavon, thank you for being great little brothers. You guys are an inspiration. You've shown me how to live life with no worries and how to just be happy.

Thank you, Isabella, for being a caring and embracing little cousin every time I visit you in Illinois. I will never forget trying to find blue jays and cardinals with you to take pictures of on those sunny summer days.

I want to thank you, Jacob, for being a great buddy and a best friend. Your presence lights up a room, and I know nothing will ever get you down.

To my readers: I hope you enjoy reading this book as much as I enjoyed writing it. It will be the first of many.

Thank you all for helping me live my life with a child's heart.

Dreaming Their Way Out

One starry night under a full moon at Saint Little's Orphanage, seven orphans were dreaming of a night when they could finally have a family and leave the terrible place they called home.

They never had any time to have fun because they were forced to do homework and clean every day. They didn't know that tonight would be the night that changed everything.

While the orphans dreamed about escaping, the moonlight shone suddenly through the skylight into their room. The light was so bright it woke them up.

At that moment the room started to shake, and silver sparkles came from the moon and flew all around them. Scared but curious, the children quickly ran to the triplets' bunk beds.

Isabella and Jacob climbed up to the top bunk to hide with Lavon. Zoey swiftly crawled from her bed to the middle bunk to hide with Liam. On the bottom bunk Arjun hid with Loyal. While they hid inside their blankets, the silver sparkles filled up the room and the shaking grew harder.

"What's going on?" Isabella asked Jacob.

"I don't know. It might be an earthquake," he replied.

Lavon gave them a funny look and said, "No way! Did you see the silver stuff coming from the moon? There's something else going on here."

All at once the room went still and the silver sparkles disappeared. When the children removed their blankets, they found that they were soaring over the clouds and across the night sky.

Arjun looked down, astonished. "I can't believe we're above the clouds," he said.

"I know! I can't even see the city from here," Loyal added.

Zoey was amazed and touched Liam's shoulder. "Look how bright the stars are and how big the moon is."

"Yeah, it looks like we're in space," Liam responded.

Ahead of them was a swarm of bright white clouds in a beautiful blue sky. The sight took their breath away.

"It looks amazing!" Isabella said.

"Where are we?" Jacob asked.

"I don't know but I think we're going to love it!" Lavon answered.

As the children laid eyes on this magical place, they saw a great ocean, an island, a beach, a jungle, and a forest loaded with snow. Zoey and Liam studied the way the land looked.

"There are so many different landscapes here," she said.

"Yes, and they all are so close together," Liam added.

All at once the bed stopped and dropped.

"Whoa!" the children yelled, as they fell through the clouds.

But as the bed came closer to the ground, it began to sway gently back and forth and slow down, and it landed softly like a feather.

On the ground, a group of people with wings surrounded the children.

Arjun was curious. "Who are you guys?" he asked.

"We are your guardian angels," one of them replied.

"How do we tell which of you is our own guardian angel?" Loyal asked.

The guardian angels each introduced themselves to their own children. Then they flew them around to see the rest of the magical world.

The triplets' guardian angels, John and Kirstie, carried them way up into the air. "Where do you want to go?" John asked.

"I don't know! We've never been here before," Lavon responded.

"John, this is their first time here. How would they know where to go?" Kirstie said. "I bet you guys would love to fly a little faster."

Liam smiled. "Yes, that would be awesome!"

"Can we fly a little higher too?" Loyal asked.

"You got it!" John replied.

Zoey's guardian angels, Michael and Shirley, took her high up into the sky to fly in and out of the clouds.

"Hold on tight, Zoey!" Michael said as she climbed on his back.

"What's that up ahead?" she asked.

"Oh that's just a rainbow," Shirley replied.

Zoey's eyes grew wide with excitement. "I've always wanted to fly through a rainbow."

"All right then, here we go!" Michael shouted while flying toward the rainbow.

Isabella's guardian angels, Jim and Nancy, flew her along a huge waterfall. She loved the feeling of the cool mist on her hands and feet.

Jim asked Isabella, "Hey, do you hear that?"

Isabella closed her eyes and listened. "Yes, what is that? It sounds like a roller coaster."

"That's the sound of the waterfall crashing into the ocean," Nancy told her.

"That's awesome!" Isabella said, keeping her eyes closed and feeling the mist.

Arjun's guardian angels, Ahmed and Jazmin, carried him up and down and all around the mountain valley.

Arjun sniffed the air. "I love this smell! It smells like spring." he said.

Jazmin laughed and said, "I love this smell too. It never gets old."

"That's true. What you smell is the lake, grass, flowers, mountains, and trees," Ahmed told him.

Jacob's guardian angels, Diego and Maria, took him across the beautiful blue ocean. As they flew close to the water, Jacob stared at his reflection.

"Do you want to touch the water?" Maria asked.

"Oh, can I?"

"Go right ahead, you'll love it," Diego told him.

When Jacob put his hands in the ocean, he felt the tiny waves brush his fingers.

Later the children had a fantastic time playing with the animals in the jungle.

"Isabella, do you want to play with the lion cubs?" Zoey asked.

"Yes, they're so cute," Isabella replied as they raced to the lions.

"Hey look, guys, I'm Tarzan!" Arjun shouted while swinging from a vine.

After laughing at Arjun, Jacob said, "When you get down from there you should try these bananas. They taste way better than Sister Agatha's food."

"Really," Liam agreed.

"Well then toss me one, please."

"Me too," Loyal said.

"Me three" said Lavon.

Loyal Zoey Jacob Isabella Liam Arjun Jovon

In the forest the children touched the snow, and it wasn't cold. Zoey wondered why. "How come the snow isn't cold?" she asked.

"It's magic," Shirley told her while cuffing the snow.

The other children and their guardians were having a snowball fight.

"Got you! I got you and you too!" Liam shouted, as he dived from tree to tree throwing snowballs at everyone.

John started balling up some snow. "Okay, now I'm going to get you," he said, flying toward Liam.

"This kid is way too fast! It's almost impossible to tag him out!" Diego said while helping Arjun make snowballs.

"I told you he's hard to get," Arjun replied.

Kirstie tried to come up with a plan. "Hey guys, let's huddle up!"

They all huddled up behind a pine tree away from Liam. "All right, what's the game plan?" Nancy asked.

"We have to completely surround him when he jumps out again."

"That's a great plan. We just have to make sure we time it perfectly," Michael told everyone.

Isabella had an idea. "I've got it! First, we should all hide. That way, when he jumps out again we can all throw snowballs at him at once."

"That's an awesome idea, Isabella," Maria said.

"Now that we have that figured out, the code word for us to throw the snowballs is Go," Ahmed told everyone.

"Okay, are we ready?" Jacob asked.

"Yes, but first let's break this huddle like they do in football games." Jim said.

Jazmin hopped into the middle and started a soft chant. "All right, *Get Liam*, on three. One . . . two . . . three!"

"*Get Liam*!" everyone whispered.

While hiding behind the trees they heard Liam crashing through the snow. When they spotted him looking for people to hit with snowballs, they surrounded him.

"GO!" Loyal shouted. They all jumped out of their hiding spots and threw snowballs at Liam.

"We finally got you!" Lavon exclaimed.

Liam nodded and laughed. "You got me," he said.

After enjoying their time in the forest, the guardians wanted to keep the children entertained, so they introduced them to a big blue whale, two dolphins, and a gigantic great blue heron.

The gigantic great blue heron flew Arjun and Loyal across the ocean as they sat on its back. "This is better than an airplane, even though we've never been on one," Arjun said.

"I know! We should definitely do this tomorrow," Loyal replied.

Liam, Lavon, and Jacob sat on the big blue whale as it powered through the strong waves across the ocean.

"Go, Big Blue, Go!" Jacob shouted.
Isabella and Zoey had a great time riding on the dolphins as they dove in and out of the water.

Later, the children were taken across the ocean to a magnificent island. There were tropical fruits everywhere and plenty of hammocks to relax on. The children ran around the island to find fruit.

"Ooh, there are pineapples here," Zoey said.

"Look, there are papayas here!" Loyal said.

"I found mangos!" Isabella shouted.

"And coconuts too," Jacob said.

After eating plenty of fruit, the children hopped onto the hammocks and dozed off. As they slept, the guardians took them back to the orphanage and wished them sweet dreams.

The next morning, the children woke up excited and talked about the wild, fun adventure they'd had in the magical world. Even though they didn't know how they'd gotten there, they were determined to go back.

Suddenly, the children's caretaker, Sister Agatha, burst through the door. "What is all this noise I hear?" she yelled.

"We're just having a great morning," Liam responded.

Sister Agatha walked over to him and said, "There will be no great mornings, not in here there won't. Now after you eat your breakfast, get to work, all of you."

After breakfast, Sister Agatha handed the
children cleaning products. "All right, you know
the drill. Wash the dishes, clean the counter,
spray the windows, and dust the bookshelves."

As they cleaned the orphanage with cheerless
faces, all the children could think about was
going back to bed.

Every night now the children could look forward to leaving the orphanage. It was fun to have a new place to call home. It was great to feel loved and appreciated by the animals and by their guardians. They cherished every moment they spent in the magical world.

One night after dinner, Sister Agatha rang her tiny gold bell and said, "Get ready for bed. You have open house tomorrow. Hopefully you'll all get adopted. That way I can get a paycheck."

That night the children gathered on the triplets' bunk beds like usual and waited for a ride back to the magical world. They waited and waited, but nothing happened. The children were very confused.

At last, their guardians appeared. "Yay!" the children shouted as they hugged them.

Jacob noticed that the guardians looked sad. "What's wrong?" he asked.

The guardians believed they had made a mistake by exposing the kids to their magical world. If the orphans were adopted, they would no longer be able to communicate with them.

"Sorry. We're afraid that you cannot come to our world anymore," Maria told the children.

"Yes, we made a mistake," Kirstie said.

"The reason we took you all to our world was so you could have some fun and leave this place for a while. I wish there was more we could do for you kids," Michael told them.

"Me too, but we have broken the guardian rules. We were not supposed to interfere with your lives to the point that you could see us," John said.

"No!" the children yelled.

"We want you in our lives," Arjun pleaded.

"Please don't leave us," Liam said with tears in his eyes.

"Don't worry, we will always be with you," Shirley replied, wiping the tears from Liam's face.

"But we won't see you," Isabella said.

"But you will feel our presence," Nancy told Isabella as she held her hands.

"And pretty soon you will be happy. A family might come and adopt you tomorrow," Jim told the children.
"We don't want another family! We want you to be our family," Lavon said.

"Yeah!" the children shouted in agreement.

The children hugged their guardians until they disappeared, and then they cried themselves to sleep.

That night, the guardians realized that it was more than just the magical world that made the children happy. The children were happy because for once they felt like they had a family.

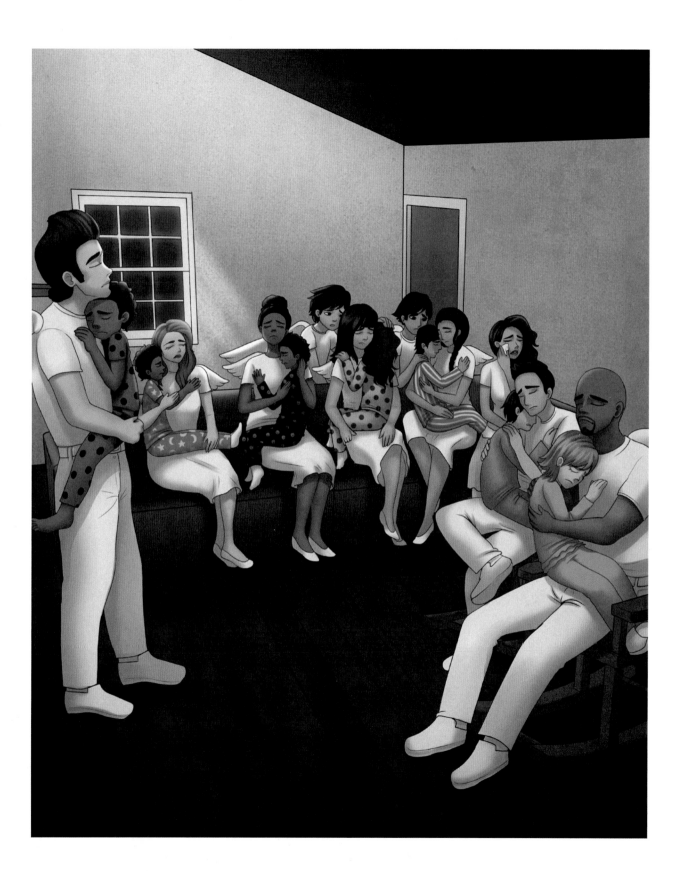

The next morning, the children woke up mopey and sad. They did not want to go through the adoption process. They just wanted to be with their guardians.

In the magical world, the guardians received a message from the sky. They had been granted a second chance at life because of their connection with the children. The guardians said goodbye to all the animals as they prepared to meet the children. Their wings and white clothing disappeared, and new clothes appeared on them.

"Hey, we look like normal people now," Diego said.

Ahmed laughed. "We look like super models."

Before they knew it, silver sparkles began flying all around them, and the ground started to shake. When it stopped and the sparkles vanished, they saw that there was nothing around them but the sky.

"Whoa!" they all screamed as they fell through the sky.

"Michael, I hope you're strong enough to catch us all before we hit the ground," Jazmin said.

"Right now I don't think that's possible," Michael replied, and everyone laughed.

At the orphanage, a few couples arrived to talk to the children.

"Hello, kids," one couple said.

"Hi," the kids replied with long faces.

"Oh come on now, brats, cheer up," Sister Agatha said. She split the children up so that the couples could talk to them one by one.

While the couples were talking to the children, the guardians were still falling through the sky. As they fell closer to the ground in front of the orphanage, they swayed back and forth like feathers until they landed on the grass. They looked around and found that they had also been granted an RV, a map, and keys to their new home.

Moments later, the guardians barged through the door with adoption papers in their hands. They called over a social worker. The children raced to their guardians and hugged them really tight and were filled with joy.

Then they saw that the guardians didn't have their wings. "What happened to your wings?" Arjun asked.

"We don't need them anymore because today we're adopting all of you," Michael whispered.

"Hey! How do you know these strangers?" Sister Agatha asked.

"Wait one minute, Sister Agatha!" the social worker said. "Thanks to these strangers, we've found out what has been going on here. These kids haven't been loved. You've been using them for labor and a payday. Your duties here are withdrawn, and we're going to finally shut down this dump."

"Yay!" the children shouted.

After reading the documents, the social worker knew the children would be in good hands and let their soon-to-be parents sign the adoption papers. They all hopped into the RV and drove to their new home.

The new house was everything the children imagined. They finally had a place to call home and could live like a true family.

To be continued . . .

Made in the USA
Monee, IL
17 September 2022

14141911R00033